BY HOWL & CLAW

5 Werewolf Stories

Rebecca M. Senese

OTHER BOOKS BY REBECCA M. SENESE

The Night Killers

The Color of Blood: The Chronicles of Richard Damon

Wreck the Halls: 5 Christmas Horror Stories

Oh the Horror! 5 Horror Stories

Bad Ends: 5 Horror Stories

With a Bite: 5 Vampire Tales

In Dwarf Land and Cannibal Country

A Very Zombie Christmas

The Beginners Guide to the Recently Deceased

Daily Bread

The In-Between Series
Book 1: A Reluctance of Blood
Book 2: A Remembrance of Flesh
*Book 3: A Retribution of Soul

*Forthcoming

BY HOWL & CLAW

5 Werewolf Stories

Rebecca M. Senese

RFAR Publishing
Toronto, Canada

Published 2015 by RFAR Publishing
Toronto, Canada
http://www.RFARPublishing.com

This is a work of fiction. All characters appearing in this work are fictitious. Any resemblance to real persons, living or dear is purely coincidental.

Trade paper edition designed by Rebecca M. Senese
in InDesign CS5.5

Electronic editions designed by Rebecca M. Senese

Cover design: Rebecca M. Senese
Cover Image © Sbelov / Dreamstime.com
Interior Images © DeCe / CanStockPhotos.com
alisher / CanStockPhoto.com

ISBN: 978-1-927603-24-6

Publications Acknowledgement

"Wild Call." First published in the *World Fantasy Convention CD-ROM*, 2001.

"These Premises Protected By..." First published in *Storyteller*, 2007.

"Wolf's Bane." First published in *Allegory*, 2010.

By Howl & Claw

5 Werewolf Stories

Table of Contents

INTRODUCTION

Welcome to *Of Howl & Claw*, a werewolf story anthology. Werewolves are not as popular as vampires but there's something interesting about werewolves. Haven't we all felt the pull of some strange urge on the night of a full moon? Werewolves speak to a wilder part of ourselves, a part that overcomes our logical, rational side and runs wild. It's the primal side under the civilized mask, or is it? Maybe it's the civilized side of us that is actually bestial. Maybe that wild wolf that races through the night is closer to our true nature.

You decide. In these stories, I take a look at werewolves and turn them on their head (or maybe their claw). Are they the beast? Or are we?

Enjoy!

Rebecca M. Senese
December 2013

A Trace Of Blood

Without a doubt, the guy was dead. It wasn't the amount of blood sprayed around the room that convinced Detective Lionel Collins, although no one could survive such a blood loss. Mostly it was the position of the corpse. Dead bodies had a unique, discarded look about them, like an empty glove. This guy was definitely empty.

He turned away from the corpse and looked around the small, ground floor bachelor apartment. Other than the blood, the place was neat. No sign of a struggle except for the broken window. It looked like someone had smashed through and sliced up the victim before he could react. Someone or something.

"Doesn't look like anything's missing," the voice of his partner, Stan Pollani broke into his thoughts. "Just like the other ones last month."

"I don't think the motive was robbery." Collins glanced back at the corpse, at the organs that erupted from the chest like the guy was a squished jelly donut. "Tell the pathologist to make sure everything is still there."

Pollani stopped jotting notes on his ever present notepad. "You think this could be some kind of cult activity? Stealing organs?"

Collins shrugged. "I don't know. But I'm pretty sure this wasn't any spat with a girlfriend."

He left his partner to supervise the bagging of the body and headed out. Fat rain drops plopped onto the sidewalk in front of him, a vague threat. The chill in the air made him hunch his shoulders;

over the past several years damp chills had caused an ache in his shoulders that he wished he could deny. Just sore muscles, he always told himself, ignoring his family history of arthritis. The arthritis had been so bad for his father that at forty-five, he could no longer do the fine finger movements required as a jewelry maker. Pain wasn't always physical.

A rain drop splattered on his forehead as he reached the car. Typical. He wiped it off and got behind the wheel. Just the thing to start the day off right. First a weird murder and now the rain. With a sigh, he started the car and pulled away.

Collins was typing up his final report when Harry Ridel wandered over to his desk with a perplexed look on his normally bland face.

Staring at the keyboard, Collins typed the three more words with two fingers and then turned to Ridel. "Hi Harry, what's up?"

Ridel settled his thin frame into the plastic chair usually reserved for suspects. "It's weird," he announced.

"What's weird?"

"These prints. I can't figure them out."

"What prints are those, Harry?"

Ridel slapped down a vanilla file in front of Collins. He flipped it open and pointed at a computer printout. "Those prints."

Collins stared at the image. It was a finger print, of a sort. The whorls and ridges looked like one but the print itself was too large for a person's finger, too elongated. Like someone had stretched their finger print, but Collins had seen smudged prints and they didn't look like this. This print was clean, no smudge.

"Where'd you get this?"

"Off that scene," Ridel said. "Your guy in the bachelor. That beauty was off the window sill and another one on the floor by the corpse." Ridel shook his head. "I hate this weird shit."

"Can't say I'm fond of it myself," Collins said. "Have you run it?"

Ridel stared at him with his overlarge brown eyes. "I can't run this, it won't match anything."

Collins sighed. Ridel was a good print man but a little lacking in imagination. If anything came outside his sphere of understanding he was stumped. "Shrink it down and then see if there's a match. If there is one, we can check it out and see how the guy does it."

Ridel closed the file and pulled it back across the desk. He still looked dubious but the wheels were slowly turning in his head. "I guess I could try that. Nothing may come up."

Collins shrugged. "And our killer may never have been printed." Ridel snorted and walked away.

It took Collins another half hour to finish typing the report but finally he was able to print it. Listening to the laser printer hiss out the pages, he slipped on his coat. He pulled the paper off the printer, stapled them and stuffed them into a folder on his desk. Ever since computers had replaced typewriters the paper in the office had tripled. So much for the rain forests.

Outside a cool wind had replaced the rain but a grey shroud still covered the sky. Winter clung with determined fingers even though it was the end of April. Collins splashed through puddles to his decaying car. He needed a new one, a fact that he was constantly reminded about by his friend Peter who ran a used car dealership. Even with the offer of a discount his pay check couldn't cover it. Carole's alimony took every extra penny he made.

Money seemed to be the only thing he'd been able to give her consistently, he thought as he headed downtown toward his small apartment. The long hours and constant stress of his job had taken their inevitable toll. Like many homicide detectives, he learned to tuck his emotions into a little corner of his mind. After a while, it became harder and harder to open up that corner after work. Carole had hung in longer than he'd expected but even with counseling, the end had been predictable.

By the time he reached his apartment, his shoulders were complaining about the chill. A long, hot shower might appease them for a while, but it looked like he'd be spending another night with the anti-inflammatories.

His answering machine blinked at him like a red, winking eye when he opened the door. His stomach tightened as he crossed to it. Not another one, he hoped.

"Hey, Lie, we're getting a game going tonight. Pete's back from out of town and his wife's at her sister's. Let the mice play! We're meeting at his place at eight. Be there with your money."

Manny Gorengo's voice cut out as the machine beeped.

It was already nine thirty. His shoulders ached. He hadn't eaten. Fatigue made him droop. All he wanted to do was grab a shower, eat some anonymous microwaved dinner and fall asleep in front of the television.

He retied the belt on his coat and left.

A chorus of shouts, groans and moans drifted out as Peter opened the door. His face was flushed and a smile spread across his cheeks. "Hi Lionel, come in. Steve just blew another hand."

As he shrugged off his coat, the men sitting in the dining room yelled their greetings. He hung up the coat and followed the sound of their voices. Peter slipped past him to reclaim his seat. He pointed at the empty chair beside him. Collins sank into it.

They'd been playing poker on and off every month since high school when Joey shoplifted a book about poker from the corner convenience. In those days, they hid out in an alley off Manny's street, using stones and bits of glass as betting chips. In university they graduated to using real poker chips, as though that bestowed a certain amount of elegance to the game. Now as they endured their forties, they'd dispensed with the false airs and used straight cash.

"Just in time to give us your money, eh Lionel?" Joey smiled as he shuffled the cards in his chubby hands. He sat on the other side of Peter. Across from Collins, Manny grinned, black wavy hair greased back as always. Steve slouched beside him, looking miserable.

"I could use a little money," Manny said.

Steve grunted.

"How bad was it?" Collins asked.

"A pair," Steve said. "Bluffed me out of a straight with a pair." He leaned his head in his hands, shaking it back and forth.

Collins felt a smile creep onto his face and his shoulders slowly loosened.

At eleven they ordered a pizza and then another one at twelve fifteen. By one, most of the damage had been done with Steve slowly winning some money back, Joey losing more and Manny turning out to be the clear winner. Both Peter and Collins managed to keep their losses under control and the game was declared a success.

In the old days, their games had dragged on to the wee hours of the morning but now they were too old and responsible for that. Everyone had jobs in the morning, including Joey who had been the true delinquent until he settled down into his father's business. Steve worked in an accounting firm in the city and Manny ran a small restaurant. Peter had inherited his father's used car dealership.

As the guys trickled out, Peter silently asked him to stay with the touch of a hand on Collins's arm. Collins watched his friends pull on their coats and leave, remembering thinner, shorter boys full of energy and enthusiasm. Could these tired, ordinary men be the same people?

"You got here late," Peter said. "You deserve to have your drink."

They wandered into the living room and Collins sat down on the couch. Peter poured cognac into two brandy snifters and handed one to Collins.

"Here's to the occasional win." Peter raised his glasses.

Collins followed suit, suddenly thinking of the dead man in his bachelor apartment. No more occasional wins for him.

After they sipped, Peter sat in the armchair opposite. "Okay, what is it? Problems in the department?"

Collins blinked. "What?"

"You've barely been here tonight. The only reason you didn't lose your shirt is because you've got such a good poker face."

"A body," Collins said. "Messy and strange."

Peter sipped his drink. "Strange how?"

"It must have happened fast because there was no sign of a struggle. And these weird long finger prints."

"What do you mean long prints?"

"Elongated." Collins gestured with his hands. "I told Ridel to run them but I don't think we'll get anything."

"Is that it?" Peter asked.

"I should think that's enough."

Peter twirled the brandy snifter. "Have you heard from Carole?"

Collins shook his head. His only contact with her was through her lawyer and that was too depressing to contemplate.

"Six months isn't very long," Peter said, addressing the living room at large.

"Right," Collins growled.

A frown spread on Peter's face, deepening the lines around his mouth until he actually looked his age. "This body's really got to you, hasn't it?"

"It's weird, like the ones last month. I don't like weird. More often than not, the weird ones don't get solved. The department won't admit it though. They just try to bury it under a pile of paper and forget it."

He blinked at the bitterness that crept into his own voice. God, he was tired. Maybe it was time for that vacation he'd been thinking about. A week or two away from the city, away from the night shift, would rejuvenate his batteries and drive out the cloud of despair. Maybe he'd pull out those brochures his partner had stuck in his desk.

Without tasting it, he drained the cognac. "Thanks for the drink, Peter, but I've got to get going."

Peter rose to walk him to the door. "Take it easy, Lionel. Don't let it get to you. You're the only sane one of the bunch of us."

Collins chuckled. "I would think that would describe you more than me, Pete."

Peter smiled and bid him goodnight.

Stan Pollani was hunting in Collins's desk for paper clips when he arrived. Pollani swore softly under his breath, a constant accompaniment to most of his activities. It was why Collins did most of the talking to witnesses.

"Any news?" Collins asked.

"Autopsy's scheduled," Pollani said. "Ridel is hunting for prints and has let it be known that he thinks it's a goddamned waste of time and resources. His phrase. The body has been positively identified as Robert Malcolm, age twenty-nine, a real estate broker. Single guy, no current girlfriend. He was last seen at eleven thirty, leaving the Stompin' Around nightclub. Nothing else until his office called because he didn't show up for work. They called the landlord and he made the discovery."

"You confirmed nothing was taken?"

Pollani flipped through his notebook. "Yep, nothing stolen. Either he interrupted before they could take anything and murdering him spooked them or they killed him for the fun of it."

"I'm betting on the latter," Collins said. "Now get the hell away from my desk."

Ridel came by later. He slapped a photocopy down on Collins's desk. "This is a copy of the shrunken finger print. Nothing comes up in our files. It was a complete waste of time."

Collins took the paper. "Thank you for your efforts. Could I get a copy of the elongated print?"

Ridel glared at him and stalked away. Behind Collins, Pollani chuckled.

"Such a pompous idiot," he said. "I don't know how you can stand to be nice to him."

"If I'm not, he'll find a way to screw things up," Collins said. He set the copy aside and continued reviewing the preliminary autopsy report.

The injuries were made by some kind of undetermined slashing instrument. Collins frowned at that. What the hell did that mean? It had to have been a knife, didn't it?

He tried calling the pathologist's office but learned the doctor was gone. Typical, he thought as he hung up the phone. It seemed like even the death doctors got out early. He fingered the report in his hand. Maybe they'd have a better idea when the full report came out. In the meantime, this was all he had.

They had traced Malcolm's movements for the last few days of his life. Nothing out of the ordinary showed up. The guy was normal, no outrageous outstanding debts. No shady connections. His love life appeared normal, his last girlfriend had been six months ago and he'd been dating a variety of women sporadically thereafter. Nothing to indicate why he would be ripped apart on a Wednesday evening.

Collins closed the report then stood up. Already seven o'clock. Time to go home. Tonight he'd get to bed early, he promised himself.

The phone jolted him awake. He fumbled for it in the dark, afraid to turn the light on and wake Carole. Only when his hands closed on the receiver did he remember that Carole was long gone.

"Collins," he barked and switched on the light.

"Lionel..." The voice was so soft he could hardly hear it.

"Who is this?"

"Help... Lionel..."

Something in the voice sounded familiar. A cadence he knew but it was so quiet he couldn't identify it.

"Who...?"

"Help... Peter."

Adrenaline slammed into Collins, forcing him bolt upright. "Peter, where are you?"

"Park, west end. Help..."

"I'm coming."

Clouds covered the night sky, blocking the full moon and robbing Collins of a clear view of the park.

Fortunately he kept a small flashlight in the glove compartment of his aging car. He checked it before he left the car, then headed down into the foliage.

The west end of the park had been left natural. That meant lots of underbrush and looming shadows. Collins picked his way carefully through decaying leaves and dirty snow. Twisting his ankle now wouldn't help Peter but he itched to go faster. Finally off to the left he saw a form on the ground. It looked like a person.

"Peter?" he whispered.

The answer was a moan. Collins crept forward. Peter lay on his side, curled into a fetal position. His clothes were torn and his shoes missing. Gently, Collins lay a hand on his arm and turned him over. In the darkness, the blood looked black.

From his rear pocket, Collins pulled out his cell phone and called an ambulance.

"Superficial wounds," the doctor said. "The kind that look worse than they are. He'll be okay in a few hours. We're giving him some blood but other than that, I just suggest bed rest and aspirin."

Collins thanked the doctor and knocked softly on the hospital room door. It was the middle of the afternoon and he hadn't slept since Peter's early morning call. From the expression on the doctor's face as he moved away, Collins probably looked worse than Peter. But he wanted to see for himself.

"Come in." The voice was weak but not as weak as on the phone. Collins went in.

Peter sat propped up in the bed by a mound of pillows. His face was pale, made paler by his blond hair. Dark circles smudged under his eyes. He smiled weakly at Collins.

"Here he is, the hero of the day."

"How are you feeling?" Collins asked.

"Like I've been mugged and left in the park for dead," Peter said. The knife wounds on his arms were bandaged in great strips like a partially clad mummy.

Collins pulled up a chair and sat down. "Do you remember what happened?"

Peter shook his head. "I was going to the drug store to pick up some stuff for Melanie. There's an all night one over on Parliament and I decided to walk over since it was mild out. I think I heard footsteps. Something hit me. I don't remember anything else."

"How much money did you have?"

"About fifty dollars in my pocket. I didn't bother with my wallet."

"Were you attacked before or after getting to the drug store?"

"I never made it to the store," Peter said. "Is this your police officer persona?" He smiled weakly to show his humour but Collins ignored it. So far the story checked out. But the park was several blocks away from the drug store. How had the mugger gotten Peter so far if he'd been incapacitated? And why?

"Do you remember seeing anyone on the street when you came out of the house?" Collins asked.

The smile slipped from Peter's face when he saw that Collins wasn't responding. "I didn't see anybody."

"Did any cars pass you, maybe slow down or stop behind you?"

"No, nothing."

"Okay, that's all for now." Collins stood up. "You look a little tired. Get some rest and I'll stop in later tonight."

"They say they might release me tonight," Peter said.

"Can I pick you up?"

"No, Melanie is coming by."

"Okay. I'll talk to you later."

"I'm sure."

A shortness echoed in Peter's words. He didn't like being interrogated but some of the elements of his story didn't add up. Collins nodded and retreated from the room. It was another case with a touch of weirdness and involving a friend. He could do without this right now.

He was heading out of the hospital when his cell phone rang.

"Lionel," Pollani's voice said. "We've got another one."

The man was big, even in the deflating effect of death. In life, he'd probably been around six four. Glass from the shattered patio doors that backed onto a small backyard and then the park beyond sprinkled his body like confetti. They glittered red, reflecting spilled blood and shredded muscles. Collins stared down at the man's face. His left cheek was torn off, hanging on his chin like a beard of skin. His throat was gone.

"Same guy again," Pollani said. Collins turned. Pollani stood by the patio door. He pointed with one gloved hand at the frame. Collins stepped closer and squinted. The print crew had been dusting already. One lone print stretched along the frame. An elongated print.

Shit, Collins thought, I hate serials.

"Make sure Ridel matches it with the other one," he said. "Take some uniforms outside and search the backyard. It's wet out there, maybe we'll get a shoe print."

Pollani made notes on his notepad and turned away, nodding.

Collins studied the door and then faced the dead man. The assailant had come through the door like it was nothing. He'd hit the man with enough force to push him across the room. The slashing was so violent the blood splatter patterns crisscrossed along the wall behind Collins.

He stepped closer, kneeling on the carpet, avoiding a blood stain. The man's right arm was mangled while the left was barely touched. His right hand lay outstretched, toward a previously beige couch. Like he was reaching, Collins thought. He looked at the couch then he looked under the couch. The knife lay in a pool of blood.

When he called the hospital, they told him Peter had been discharged earlier in the evening. Collins thanked them and drove to Peter's house. His knuckles were white against the steering wheel.

He had to ring the bell twice before he heard shuffling footsteps in the foyer. Peter opened the door. He bent forward like an old man, his hair tousled, his face still pale. He looked surprised.

"Lionel, come in."

"Where's Melanie?" Collins stepped past Peter and into the living room.

"She had an exam in the class she's taking tonight. I told her to go. It's the final and I didn't want her missing it because of this."

"How are you feeling?"

"Still a little sore and tired. The pain killers take off the edge though. Can I take your coat?"

Collins shook his head. "I'll just leave it on," he said. "I have a couple of questions."

"Fine." Peter limped over to the couch and sat down slowly.

"You had to go to the drug store last night. The 24 hour one on Parliament, is that right?" Collins said.

Peter frowned, puzzled. "Yes."

"It isn't 24 hours anymore. It closes at midnight now. Has for the past two months. There's a big sign in the front of it advising people of the change. Isn't that the way you drive to work?"

"Yeah, so I never noticed it. Is that a crime?"

"Your clothes were torn," Collins pressed on, "and your shoes were missing. What kind of shoes were you wearing?"

"Runners, I think," Peter said. "Jesus, Lionel,

what the hell is going on? I was the one who was mugged."

"What happened to your shoes?" Collins asked. "Did the mugger take them?"

"I don't know."

"You don't remember."

"That's right, I don't remember."

"Maybe you'll remember this."

Collins tossed the plastic bag onto the coffee table between them. It landed with a small thud. The inside of the bag was coated red but it was still clear enough to see the knife.

"Do you remember this knife, Peter?"

Peter leaned forward, wincing once. He studied the knife then looked up at Collins. "Where did you get this?"

"Is this the knife that cut you?" Collins asked. "Is that your blood on it?"

Confusion settled on Peter's face. "I don't know. It could be. Where did you find it? Did you catch the guy?"

"It was at a murder victim's house," Collins said. His voice was flat. "He used it in self defense but it didn't work. Whoever killed him ripped him apart."

Peter stared at him. Astonishment and fear warred on his face, making his body quiver. "You think I did it," he whispered.

Collins shook his head. "I don't think you did, I know you did. It stops now, Peter. I can't cover up for you again."

Peter trembled. His hands grasped his knees but they still shook. "I didn't," he said. "I've got control. The farm..."

"It isn't enough. Not any more. Goats and sheep were never your first choice. You told me you could guarantee you'd only hunt them but you can't even remember what you did last night."

"It wasn't me." Peter struggled to stand. One hand reached for the couch arm for support. As it did so, the fingers began to stretch, the nails began to grow.

Collins stepped back. His hand went to his holster. "Stay where you are, Peter. I don't want to fire."

As the nails grew, the couch fabric puckered then tore. Peter hunched more, this time from the changes taking place in his body. A moan came from his mouth as his face stretched into a muzzle. His lips tried to form words, but only gurgles sounded. He took a step forward, then another.

Collins drew his gun. Slowly he retreated toward the door. "Peter, you're under arrest for murder. With your condition, you could plead temporary insanity. They could help you in the hospital. Are you listening, Peter?"

The answer was a snarl as the beast, unleashed by extreme stress, revealed itself. It hunched down and sprang. Collins's answer was a gun shot.

He couldn't bear to face Melanie so Pollani intercepted her and told her the news. Her vehement denials turned to tears. The elongated fingerprints didn't match Peter's exactly but it was close enough. In death, Peter had regained his human form.

Collins followed the body out to the ambulance and then watched it drive away. His empty holster flapped under his arm; Pollani had taken the gun as evidence. There would be questions but the blood on the knife and the shoe prints in the backyard of the latest victim would prove Collins right. It left a bitter taste in his mouth.

He turned one last time to look at the house and saw Melanie standing in the doorway. Grief twisted her face, her eyes squinting. Her hair hung in strings around her face. Her hand on the door knob shook. Her mouth opened once, then closed with a snap. She turned and walked deeper into the house. Collins felt the blow as though she had slammed the door in his face. He got the hell out of there.

The next shift stretched endlessly with constant questions and reviews of his reports. Collins endured it, his face a mask. That tiny corner where he shoved his emotions started to bulge and push at the boundaries of his mind. He kept seeing Peter struggling to rise from the couch, his hand changing. Somewhere in his mind he had known, as far back as high school and the tales about the big, black dog that roamed the streets of the neighbourhood. But he had denied it; he was so good at denial. He only had to ask Carole.

He finally made it home just before nine. The sun, what little there was of it, was already down. His apartment was a hole of darkness. He welcomed it, quiet and soothing. Maybe it would still the turmoil in his head.

After contemplating a microwave dinner for about five seconds, he headed straight for the bedroom. He felt like he could sleep for years. Exhaustion lay heavy on his bones. Slowly he peeled his clothes off before collapsing under the sheets and closing his eyes to the hard reality of his life.

He came awake to a warm, wet wind blowing on his face. He thought of the pond in the old neighbourhood, and then opened his eyes.

The window was wide open, the curtains blowing inward like flags. He tasted the ripeness of the decaying leaves and fresh dirt. And the warm, wet breath of something alive.

Melanie towered above him. He recognized the necklace, the torn remnants of a skirt. Her blouse was entirely gone, revealing a chest of brown fur that was nowhere near human.

"Wrong guess," she growled, leaning forward until her wide muzzle was an inch from his nose. His heart quivered in his chest, afraid to pound. He sat frozen. His gun, returned that afternoon, was in the living room. No possible chance of reaching it.

"Think you're clever? Not by a long shot." Her hand slashed out, claws extended. Pain pierced his face as his cheek ripped open. He felt her tongue on his skin, sucking up the blood. He could taste death in his mouth. He closed his eyes.

She was gone. Her footsteps backed away and then the wind from the open window reached him. Collins opened his eyes. The room was empty. He staggered to his feet and to the window.

She was disappearing behind a building two blocks away. He had to stop her. He stumbled into the living room, looking for his gun. Why had she left him alive when she slaughtered the others? That didn't matter. He had to catch her before she killed again.

He found the holster on the table beside the couch. In the darkness, he fumbled with the snap, having trouble. Impatiently, he turned on the lamp to see better. Yellow light pierced the darkness, showing him the buckled holster and his hands as they slowly began to stretch, the nails beginning to grow.

Collins opened his mouth to scream but all that came out was a howl.

Wild Call

During the long hours of summer sunshine Buck searched for gold. His sled dogs, so thin when they finally managed to get to Stewart in the late spring, now romped among the brittle summer grass. When he called them in to eat, he admired the return of the healthy sheen of their coats. Muscles, once stringy from the hardships of winter, drew firm and strong again. When he was finished with them, he knew he'd get a good price for them in Dawson.

Meanwhile, he spent his day working the river as he waited for his partner Henry to return with more provisions. Henry had taken their second dog team to sell. He would then return on his own with some promised luxuries.

The search for gold was slow and back breaking, but Buck didn't mind. The sun warmed his face. The fresh scent of wild flowers and grass rode the breeze. In the evenings he stretched out beside the small crumbling log cabin Henry had found to watch the sun slowly moving across the sky. It felt odd to have the sun shining down so late at night. Often he'd shake himself to find it was almost midnight and well time he got to sleep. Strange to sleep when the sun still shone, but he knew as the summer waned, the cold darkness would return, slowly creeping to claim the frozen heart of this northern land.

He wanted to be gone before that happened, back to the bustle of San Diego where Sadie waited. She was patient but her father was not. He could all but see the old man's disapproving face in Sadie's last letter. If he and Henry managed to hit a large strike, that old man's disapproval would vanish. No, not if. When. It would happen.

He worked the river extra hard that afternoon.

The dogs barking finally reminded him to feed them. He was surprised to find it was after eight. The dogs trailed him back to the cabin, dancing on frantic legs until he tossed a fish to each of them. He and Henry had agreed to continue the food rationing. Now that they were settled, the dogs could hunt for extra food if they wanted it. It gave them good exercise and kept them sharp.

After feeding the dogs, he fed himself but it was mostly by rout. He didn't taste any of the mush. Instead he stared at the sky, watching the sun in the seemingly eternal bright sky.

That evening he went to bed early and put a strip of cloth over his eyes to block the sunlight. Already he could feel the nights becoming cooler although it was still only the beginning of September. They had a huge stash of wood by the side of the cabin but he should collect more scrub and twigs for kindling. He'd start that in the morning. Planning his day, he fell asleep...

And woke to howling.

The darkness disoriented him. He'd forgotten what it was like, so used to the sun. For a moment, he was back in San Diego, in the filthy room off the alley and the howl was a fight outside. Then he remembered. The Yukon, and the howl was a wolf.

The dogs were snarling, crying out. Buck stumbled out of bed, grabbing for the rifle. The darkness tripped him up, hid the rifle, then reluctantly released it as Buck's eyes adjusted. By the time he threw the door open, he could see.

He fired a shot into the sky. Most times, the noise scared a pack off. The dogs yelped, rushed the cabin. Buck pushed through, waving the rifle, yelling. He couldn't see the wolf pack, just that incessant howling. It sounded like it came from everywhere.

His foot slipped and he fell. The rifle jolted from his hand, landed a few feet away. He scrabbled for it and stopped, seeing a thin wolf-like shadow. It pounced on top of one of the smaller dogs, Slade. Slade yowled, shoulder torn open to the bone. The dog staggered, fell. The wolf, all bone and snarl, jumped forward, slashing open Slade's throat then bounced away. Buck watched, hypnotized as the dog's jerking body spasmed one final time and lay still.

Then he felt the wolf eyes turn to him, staring. That cold, harsh glare sized him up, measuring the distance to strike. The rifle was between him and the wolf. A few feet. Could have been a few miles, a few hours. The wolf head dipped. One paw stepped forward. No howling now. Even the dogs behind him were quiet. Expectant. Only a few feet.

He dove for the gun as the wolf leapt. Now it snarled, a loud roar. He felt its breath on his face, hot and wet. Its spit dotted his face. No time for aiming. He pulled the trigger. The roar of the gun undercut his own shriek of pain as claws tore his left shoulder.

The wolf fell away. No triumphant leap aside. It landed in a heap, moaning. Buck dragged himself back. Let the dogs finish it. His shoulder ached where the wolf had slashed him. Using the rifle as a crutch, he pulled himself to his feet and staggered back toward the cabin. The dogs moved forward, dark shadows. He heard them growling as he shut the cabin door.

He lit a lamp to see that his left shoulder was worse than he'd thought. Blood streamed down his arm and soaked his pants. He used his sleeping cloth dunked in water to wipe the worst of it away. The slashes were deep, difficult for him to tend to alone. He pulled out his only clean shirt and used it to bind his shoulder. He tied it with rope, as tight as he could, his breathing hissing out with the pain. Henry was due back any day now. Would probably come walking back into the camp tomorrow and he would know what to do. Henry was always on about healing potions, he would have something to help for sure.

Buck concentrated on that, pushing any fear far back into his mind. He didn't have to worry now. The wolf was dead. The dogs had finished it off; he still heard them snarling outside. Sleep began to overtake him even as he sat down on the bed. He allowed it to pull him down, obliterating the final, lingering question in his mind.

Wolves hunted in packs. So where was the pack?

In the morning, his shoulder had stiffened and he could barely get out of bed. Finally he rolled onto his right side and pushed himself up. The dull ache told him he had at least survived the night.

Outside, the thought of food made his stomach churn but he forced himself to drink water. A patch of damp ground was the only trace left of the wolf. Buck sat down to rest after the effort of leaving the cabin. So much for working the river today.

Despite the sunshine, the air was chilled and Buck knew the summer was ending. Already he could tell the sun was not as powerful as before. Here at the top end of the world, day and night battled savagely for dominion. The reign of day was slowly coming to an end and night would soon be supreme.

Buck did not want to be around for that but his wounded shoulder threatened his plans. With Henry slow to return, the envisioned strike before winter dimmed. They might have to struggle through another six months which meant hanging on to the dogs and fighting to survive here. He knew he could do it, had done it, but wanted to be gone. He'd had enough of this land. He wanted a soft bed to sleep in, wanted to wake up to a hot fresh meal and see Sadie's smile. He pushed the thoughts away. No use dwelling. If Henry arrived soon then they might just make it back.

The sun inched across the sky and his shoulder ached. He kept thinking he should eat something but couldn't bring himself to do it. Once he bit off a mouthful of dried venison only to heave it back up. The only thing he could keep down was water and only that in little sips.

He spent the day watching the sun and the dogs. They romped around the cabin, pausing occasionally to look at him curiously. Usually he went down to the river and they were confused by the disrupted routine. Several times they came up to him to be fed but he shooed them away.

Henry didn't return that day, so Buck finally fed the dogs then retired to the cabin early. He sipped more water and again thought about food but couldn't muster enthusiasm for it. He lay down on the piled blankets. The sun still filtered through the slats of the cabin so he again placed the cloth strip across his eyes. Even as his hand fell back, he was asleep.

He dreamed of the forest, of moving through the trees in the darkness. The air was crisp and cold, the ground crunched beneath his feet. Up ahead he could smell prey, food, waiting for him to catch it. He heard the call, felt the vibration of it in his bones and it filled him with a desire stronger than he had ever known. Eagerly he moved through the woods, wanting to rush but knowing that loud noise would flush out the prey too quickly. But even as he thought it, he felt the prey move farther away and he gave chase.

Cold air filled his lungs as he ran through the forest. The wind howled around him, carrying him forward. He shouted out his own answer, his own excitement as he ran and it came echoing back through the trees. He knew he would catch the prey, knew he was gaining by each step. The trees flashed by. He pushed himself forward, felt his heart pounding, his blood warming him even in the freezing air. He shouted his imminent triumph to the wind and it howled back. The ground sloped and curved. The trees gave way to a small clearing and he could almost see his prey...

The dogs barking woke him. The morning had come awfully suddenly. Buck's shoulder throbbed as he pushed himself up and staggered out of the cabin. The dogs impatiently danced around, darting forward and back. What was the matter with them? He'd just fed them last night. He glanced into the sky and stopped.

The sun. It was in the wrong place. Had the world suddenly reversed it rotation? It should be rising.

He'd slept the entire day. Numbly, he tossed fish to the dogs then sat down on the log outside the cabin. How could he have slept the entire day? The wound had made him sleepy that he was sure of, but he'd never heard of a man having to sleep the entire day. He must have needed it. That much was obvious. Perhaps it would heal faster and he could get back to working the river again. Maybe by the time Henry returned, he would almost be back to normal.

Again he tried to eat and although he was hungry, he couldn't keep the food down. It tasted odd to him so he spat it out. Instead he continued to sip water as he sat up and watched the sun.

After a few hours he was tired. He dragged himself back into the cabin and noticed that the sun was lower than the night before. Full darkness was advancing on a daily basis now.

His dream took him back to the forest. He could see the trees more easily now and they looked different from the ones he knew. These were immensely old, suggesting a different time, a more ancient time. In this forest, no man had ever walked before. The howls he heard were from some long extinct beast. Hearing it stirred his blood, made his heart beat faster. It was the call of prey, the call to hunt and feed. He took off through the forest, chasing the howl.

The next day he again woke too late to do any work at the river. He fed the dogs and sat in front of the cabin, watching the sun, waiting. The throb of his shoulder was duller now and he removed the bloodied shirt to look at the wound. Crusted blood sealed it shut. He wrapped a rag soaked in water over the sight, wincing at the slight pain. As far as he could tell there was no infection. It would heal, leaving him with a long scar. It would probably ache when it rained, he thought. He considered food but it held no interest for him. He kept sipping water.

That night he stayed up, not tired. All the sleep he'd had left him restless but he couldn't work the river, didn't want to do it. He paced back and forth along the length of the cabin, five steps one way, four steps the other. The space was small and felt smaller by the second. Finally he left to stand outside.

The sun was almost down and darkness was creeping forward. Around him, the dogs were curled up asleep. Several twitched as they romped in their dreams. Buck walked over to the fire pit and kicked at the ash pile. He was hungry. He should start up a fire and cook something. He felt like he could gorge himself tonight. This was a good sign; his shoulder must be healing if his appetite had returned. He began to gather kindling to build a fire, but even as he lit it and nurtured the fire, his interest in food waned.

He didn't want to cook. He tried to think of all the meals he could have back in San Diego; thick, juicy steaks and large baked potatoes. Steaming lobster with fresh vegetables. The memories did nothing for him. He stamped the fire out and stirred the ashes. Best not to waste wood or kindling on a fire he wouldn't use.

Might as well go back to sleep, he thought, but he didn't want to. Around him, the trees blended into the darkness and instead of being as menacing as before, they seemed to invite him. He felt a stirring to go walk among them. Hadn't he dreamt of trees? He couldn't remember. Something about running, a howl calling him forward. It was dangerous to leave the cabin at night. The wolf attack several nights ago underlined the danger that lurked in that darkness but still he felt drawn forward. The urge to run made the muscles in his legs twitch. He stepped closer, watching the trees spread their branches open in welcome.

The skin in his shoulder itched as a cold breeze blew over him. He could almost hear something in the wind, a hint of prey and it stirred him. He moved faster into the trees. The crunch of the ground beneath his feet was loud. He could suddenly hear everything in the forest. The sway of the branches over his head, the rustle of the brush, the scurrying feet of some nearby animal. He paused, listening harder for it. Off to his left. He turned to follow.

The scurrying sounded louder as he drew near. Crouching, he peeked over a bush and saw a rabbit digging at the hard ground. It froze, then lifted its head, ears wide and listening. Buck held his breath. After a moment, the rabbit bent back to its task, scratching at the ground with its paws. Buck crouched lower, gathering his strength for one quick rush. He waited another moment, listening to the rabbit scrape. He shot forward.

Outreached hands missed the rabbit by inches. Startled, it leapt away and ran. Buck raced after it. The cold air stabbed his lungs, blasted his shoulder. He gulped air, felt his blood boil as he ran. Running through the forest he felt completely free. Each footfall was sure. He didn't worry about stumbling. He leapt through the trees as if he knew the way. He felt fully alive, fully aware of the prey racing away from him. He knew he would catch it, could almost feel his teeth sinking into the soft flesh, taste the rush of blood into his stomach, filling it, filling him. He would gorge in it, revel in his kill and howl his pleasure to the night sky.

Around a grove of trees, he saw the rabbit scurrying across a small clearing. He charged after it, narrowing the space. In the darkness, its fur looked silver, reflecting ambient light. He focused on the straining haunches and leapt forward.

His hand grabbed a leg and he held on. The rabbit screamed, scrambling to escape. Buck dragged it back and with a billow of triumph, sank his teeth into the rabbit's throat. It shrieked, the sound vibrating in his mouth as he chewed. He felt the body jerk and grow still. His hunger enveloped him and he tore savagely at the carcass.

As he licked the blood from his nails, a howl rose around him and he lifted his face to the sky, not aware that his mouth was open and his voice joining the call.

The sun made Buck blink. Had he left the cabin door open to let the strong sun shine through? He opened his eyes.

Trees surrounded him. He bolted up. Where was he? His hands were dirty with dried blood. Around him, bones and fur littered the ground. He stared at it, uncomprehending. Then memories came slowly back. The rabbit. The chase. The capture. His stomach lurched. He'd eaten the thing live.

It was hunger, he told himself, only hunger. After three days of course he'd been starved and acted like a madman. Who wouldn't? He stumbled back toward the cabin. He felt stronger now, better. He could return to working the river and wait for Henry. Then when Henry arrived, they could leave for good. He no longer cared if they found a rich strike of gold.

Through the day he forced himself to work the river, to return to his regular routine. But when it came time to feed the dogs, they wouldn't come near him, wouldn't take the fish he offered. He tossed it toward them but they whined at him and backed away. He shouted at them impatiently and one of them snarled. The sound enraged him and he leapt at the dog. His hands grabbed the muzzle and a front leg. Startled, the other dogs fled. The one in his hands tried to pull away. He snarled and sank his teeth into its fleshy throat.

Blood gushed into his mouth, igniting euphoria. It blazed within him as surely as the night overtook the day. All thoughts of leaving disappeared the same way the sun sank beneath the distant horizon. Soon the night spread across the land and Buck moved out into the forest to hunt the rest of the dogs down.

Two days later as the sun set early in the afternoon, Henry arrived at the camp. With a grunt, he dumped the pack off his back and dropped the lead of the small sled he'd been dragging. The camp was quiet and he thought that maybe Buck was down by the river working. He stowed the pack in the cabin and stepped outside, stretching his arms.

"Hey, Buck," he called. "You at the river? Where are the dogs?"

Silence answered him. It seemed odd that not one of the dogs had come at the sound of his voice to investigate. He glanced around and slowly noticed the small signs of disuse. The fire pit held a bare scattering of ashes. Bones littered the ground. He looked back at the cabin and remembered how the door had been open when he arrived.

Henry went to retrieve the rifle from his pack in the cabin. Inside, he noticed the disarray of the cabin. Buck had always been meticulous in his neatness. Packed a sled up neat, kept the cabin neat, because you might need something in a hurry and it should be where you need it. But now the cabin was a mess. The few pieces of clothing not tore into shreds were strewn across the floor. A single bottle of scotch lay in the centre, its liquid long drained away.

Something had happened. Indians maybe, Henry thought, but he'd never seen anything like this. Quickly, he loaded the rifle. By the time he left the cabin the sun was already down, leaving a last few streaks of orange across the cold, clear sky.

Damn, he couldn't go looking in the forest now. He set the rifle down against the cabin and gathered kindling to make a fire. A healthy pile of brush and twigs caught easily and soon he had a good blaze going. From the trees, he heard a twig snap, or was it from the fire? He peered out into the darkness but the brightness of the fire made it difficult to see. Was something out there? Maybe one of the dogs. If that were so, it would come to the fire, so maybe it was a wolf.

Henry reached for the rifle lying against the cabin wall.

Something howled and knocked him sideways. The rifle fell out of reach. He twisted away, toward the fire. The creature snarled in anger and darted back. Henry grabbed for the rifle, but the creature lunged forward, kicking it away.

Claws dug into his chest, shredding skin. Henry gasped in air, struggled to hit back. He stared up at the thing attacking him. Was it a wolf? No, it couldn't be. Not the way it held him down. Then he saw. A face, oh god, it was a face!

"Buck," he cried. There was still something of a man in that face although the lower jaw stretched forward into a crude muzzle. The mouth opened to reveal gleaming fangs. Brown hair covered powerful shoulders that withstood any pounding.

"Stop please," Henry said but the only answer was a bellowing howl. Instead of ripping out his throat, Buck's jaws clamped onto Henry's upper arm. Henry screamed as teeth sank into his flesh. He struggled to pull away, when Buck released his grip.

Henry struggled to focus on the creature that stepped back into the darkness but the pain overwhelmed his senses. He passed out.

When he awoke the sun was low in the sky. He thought it was rising but it was in the wrong part of the sky. How had he slept the entire day?

Movement caught his attention. Buck emerged from the trees, moving on all fours. His form blended into the encroaching darkness. Henry tried to speak but couldn't summon the strength. His chest was soaked with blood. His arm ached. Would Buck kill him now? Why hadn't he been killed already?

As the sun sank lower, Buck seemed to expand to fill the distance between the camp and the trees. His breathing echoed so loudly it drowned out the roaring of Henry's blood. It sounded like a howl. Inside Henry, something stirred. He felt pulled toward that call. He stared harder into the darkness, trying to see Buck, trying to will him closer.

When Buck finally lifted his voice to howl into the sky, Henry opened his mouth to join him.

THESE PREMISES PROTECTED BY...

"I told you the back door was the easiest," Denny Wilson said, drawing the kitchen shades. "I've been walking this neighbourhood for months."

His partner, Billy Wayne Benton, stood inside the door, his hefty six foot four inch frame hiding the ruined door jam. He hated when Denny bragged about his methods, especially during a job. Excess talking was sloppy, a sign of inferior thinking. Billy didn't talk unless absolutely necessary.

This habit suited Denny perfectly. His short, lithe body skimmed across the tile floor and he peeked into the dining room. More windows, these blinds drawn but not totally closed.

"Wait here," he told Billy. He could see the man nod impatiently, a flicker of distaste crossing his face. Denny grinned. He loved to needle the big, silent man.

He toured the bottom floor of the house, posh living room, exquisite dining room, crisp office/den. Taping the edges of the shades with masking tape, he mumbled as the double thick gloves stuck on the tape. He'd read once that cops could get prints through thin gloves and he'd doubled up ever since.

Finishing, he returned to the stark, white kitchen where Billy waited.

"All ready, your highness."

Billy snorted and pushed past him, one hand brushing Denny's sleeve. Denny noticed that his glove was thin. Obviously Billy hadn't read the same article.

They worked methodically, room by room. Denny stacked stereo equipment by the back door. He preferred taking everything out to the van at once, instead of piecemeal as they went along. It was cleaner, neater. Looked more like a move than a robbery.

The sound of drawers opening told Denny that Billy was in the dining room. The big man definitely had a flare for silver, being able to distinguish the real thing from cheap stainless steel with barely a glance. It almost made up for his personality, his brooding silences and nasty glares. They'd never be friends but Denny knew the value of a working relationship.

The 42 inch LCD panel television proved too heavy for him to lift. He retreated to the office/den where Billy was rifling a rollup desk.

"Can you get the TV?" Denny said. "Too heavy for me."

Billy nodded, a sharp movement of his large head. His hair, cut to an inch, barely shifted. He eased the cover down and slipped out from behind the desk. He had remarkably grace for all his bulk. Denny remembered how he had elegantly pulverized the biker at the bar last Wednesday who kept interrupting their final plans for this job.

Of course, such bulk made Billy stand out, made him noticeable in a crowd, around a neighbourhood. He couldn't pick houses for himself. That was Denny's job. Nondescript, inconspicuous Denny, who could fit in with mechanics or bankers, depending on his clothes and attitude. His mother's always said he could've been a great actor, just like Sir Larry, but Denny knew just how much most actors ever made.

Forget that.

With a grunt, Billy hefted the LCD panel television. He inched toward the doorway. Denny stepped out into the hallway watching. Billy's feet sank into the plush white carpet as he moved forward, his thick treads leaving deep marks like a golfer's treads in virgin green.

"Easy now," Denny murmured.

Billy stepped into the hallway, heading for the kitchen two dozen or so paces away. Denny tiptoed behind.

Almost to the kitchen, he was breathing a sigh of relief. Billy moved confidently, now used to the television's weight. He strode down the hallway and as one foot stepped onto the kitchen tile, the other, resting on the carpet, began to rise. Suddenly his foot pulled back, slipping on the rug. With a yell, the big man began to fall. He twisted, arms pushing the television away. The unit hit the wall with a crash as the screen exploded. Billy landed on his side, his face a few inches from the ruined set.

"Shit, Billy." Denny rushed forward, reaching down to help the big man stand but Billy slapped his hands away. Billy's face was blotchy and red.

"Why'd you pull at the carpet?" he growled.

"What? What the hell are you talking about? I didn't pull at the carpet. You slipped."

"The carpet was pulled out from under my foot," Billy roared.

"Shut up, you want the neighbours to hear you?" Denny shook his head. "Why the hell would I pull the carpet? You think I wanted to destroy the television? That's three maybe four hundred dollars gone. Do I look stupid?"

Slowly the colour settled in Billy's face. He glared at the offending carpeting. One foot poked at it cautiously.

"Look it's just carpet. We're lucky the screen didn't land on you."

Billy grunted.

"Come on," Denny urged. "Let's finish up this floor. Forget that." He gestured vaguely to the ruined tv.

They abandoned the television in the hallway, retreating to the office. Billy returned to the rollup desk, absently rubbing his hip. Denny scanned the bookshelves that flanked the heavily curtained window. After a moment, he noticed how many of the books dealt with parapsychology. Jez, these people actually had the whole Time/Life set. He remembered watching those stupid commercials at four in the morning, nursing the beginnings of a hangover.

He tapped one of the bindings. "Hey, Billy, what's lycanthropy?"

"Werewolves," Billy murmured.

Denny snorted. "Like 'American Werewolf in London'". He'd liked that movie, funny. These people seemed to actually believe it. Some people believed anything these days.

His fingers explored the bindings of the books and sure enough, a different kind of pressure on the shelf just above his head. He grabbed a handful of books and tossed then to the floor. Groping around on the shelves, his fingertips brushed the sharp edges of paper. He grabbed and pulled out a large brown envelope. Bingo, the family cookie jar. He ripped open the envelope and rifled through the bills, mostly twenties. Just over five hundred, he figured. Rainy day money. Sorry, folks, it just started pouring.

He turned to wave the money at Billy. A scrapping sound made him hesitate. He started to turn back.

A book smacked him hard on his head.

Yelping, Denny jumped back. The book landed on the grey carpeting, pages splaying open. His head was sore where the book hit him, already he could feel a bruise starting.

"Son of a bitch," he said, rubbing the spot.

"You should be more careful how you treat books," Billy said wryly as he stooped to pick up the money Denny had dropped.

"How could that hit me?" the little man said. He glanced back at the bookcase.

"You must have moved it too close to the edge." Billy stuffed the bills back into the envelope and folded it. As Denny watched, the envelope disappeared inside Billy's jacket. Denny started to protest but then thought better of it. Billy was almost a foot taller and at least forty pounds heavier than he was. Besides, cheating your partner was not good business, it got you a reputation and soon no one would work with you. Billy was too smart to make that mistake.

"Anything in the desk?" he asked.

Billy shook his head. "Just papers, family records. Nothing for us."

"Let's check the upstairs."

They moved up the stairs, Denny trailing one hand along the polished wooden banister. Very elegant looking, he thought. But he couldn't really appreciate it. His head was starting to throb from where the book hit him. Maybe he'd find some aspirin in the bathroom medicine cabinet.

"Let's get the jewelry first," he said to Billy. "We can get the portable stereos and shit later."

Billy's curt nod was his only answer as they moved to the master bedroom. After Denny taped the curtains shut, Billy slipped over to the dresser, his big hands plunging into the jewelry box.

Denny started over to help but got distracted by a large full year calendar tacked up to the closet door. That looked odd. Most people kept this sort of thing in a den or something. He traced the dates with one gloved hand. Three or four days were circled in red every month, notations made for each one: "Grandma's," "Holiday Inn," "McGregor's," "Bed and breakfast." Looks like they go away every month, he thought. He should copy down the dates. In six months or so, after the insurance claims were settled, they could return. The cops would tell the residents that robbers won't return and then he and Billy could strike again.

He pulled out an old bus schedule and started scribbling down dates. After a few, he noticed a pattern.

"Hey Billy," he called. "Look at this. These people go away every month on the full moon. Maybe one of them is a werewolf."

A rare grin broke through the usual bland expression on Billy's face. He lifted a gold chain and wagged it at Denny. "I might've known, none of this stuff is silver."

Denny chuckled. He liked that. After copying a few more dates, he stuffed the schedule back into his pocket. While Billy finished with the jewelry box, dumping selected items into a canvas bag, Denny commenced to scour the drawers. Systematically, he pulled out every drawer and dumped the contents on the bed. Clothes mostly, with little bags of pot pourri to smell it up nicely. He turned over the drawers, looking for anything taped to the bottom. He'd broken into one place and found money taped to the bottom of every drawer in the bureau and ever since then he checked methodically.

Nothing. Should've known. He left the drawers and the mound of clothes on the bed. He opened the closet door, barely glancing at the yearly calendar. He was stretching his thin frame to its full height when the lights went out.

"What the hell?" Billy's voice snarled in the sudden darkness. Denny couldn't see anything. He couldn't have done that good a job taping the curtains to the wall. Surely a sliver of light would get in from the streetlights outside. But the darkness was heavy and oppressive, pressing against him even though he knew the bedroom was large, the furniture widely spaced.

"Probably some kinda timer," he said, louder than necessary just to hear his own voice. Billy, he knew, was across the room, but other than the first exclamation he couldn't detect the big man's presence.

Carefully Denny stretched out his hand, feeling the closet door under his fingertips. He followed it along to the wall and used the wall to lead him to where he thought the door should be. Naturally he'd left his flashlight downstairs. He could picture it sitting on the kitchen counter beside the backdoor. Shouldn't be too hard to get but he cursed the amount of time this would take up. He wanted to be out of here before sunrise.

The wall felt like some kind of stucco, scrapping against his fingertips. Jesus, it was taking a long time to get to the door. Had he turned the wrong way and was heading toward the bed? Just his luck, he'd end up banging his shins and have to turn around to start again.

"Hey Billy, I'm going for the flashlight," he said. Nothing came back out of the darkness. No noise, no feeling of movement. Had Billy gone ahead and left the room already? No, impossible, he would hear the big man's plodding footsteps down the stairs. But the darkness was perfectly silent, absorbing the sound of his movements like a drop of water into a well. It pressed against him, making it hard to breathe except in shallow, short gasps. Where the hell was Billy, he wondered. When would he reach the door?

He wasn't going to panic, he told himself. He was a professional, he'd picked locks in darkness like this, worked jobs in minimal light. He'd never had a problem with darkness, not even as a kid, and he wasn't about to have one now.

Purposely, he took a step and then another. He was probably right by the door now, any minute he'd feel the frame beneath his questing fingers. Any second.

His trailing fingers suddenly sank into something wet and lumpy. What? Oatmeal, was the first thought in his mind, dredged up from some long forgotten motherly attempt by his aunt to feed him. But that was impossible, he was touching the wall.

Maybe some weird renovation, he thought. Never mind that there hadn't been anything wrong with the wall when he'd walked in with Billy, never mind that it didn't make sense for a wall to suddenly turn fluid. He wouldn't allow for any other thought.

Keep going, there'll be drywall. He pulled his hand out of the muck, letting his fingertips brush lightly along. The door, he was heading for the door.

Then the carpeting beneath his feet felt strange. It had been a grey, tight weave with an abstract etched design working through it. Ordinary, barely noticeable. Firm beneath his shoes. Except now it felt squishy, like he was walking across the surface of a waterbed filled with gelatin. He could feel it move beneath his feet, rolling first to the right and then the left. Balancing became a new trick but still he kept trying to walk forward. It was just the darkness making him edgy, that was all.

But no matter what happened, he did not want to fall over.

Slowly he became aware that the darkness was no longer completely silent. A low creaking, just on the edge of hearing, had started. He couldn't tell where it was coming from, it seemed to hang in the air around him.

"Billy," he called. The word was swallowed by the darkness, by the rising sound that now sounded like the wind or a moan. Yes, that was it. A low moan. Could it be Billy? He strained to listen to it, to distinguish anything meaningful from it. But nothing occurred to him, except the hollow sinking feeling of decay.

Stop it, he told himself. It's just the wind slipping in through a loose window or something. The floor was solid and so was the wall. He'd reached the door any second now.

The moan rose, changing pitch, becoming sharp and harsh, gaining volume, sounding like... like...

A howl.

A high pitched shriek cut across the howl and loud thumps sounded off to his left. Suddenly the wall was gone, not even the mushy oatmeal-like texture anymore. Denny felt the door frame at his fingertips and he clung to it.

"Billy," he cried. The howl swallowed his words, the sound shaping around it to mock him. Then the lights sprang on, full brightness, blinding him. He rubbed at his eyes, tears leaking from the corners. The howl screeched in his ears, rising to a wail.

Billy!

Still blinking, Denny opened his eyes. The stairs on the right curved downward, their edges sharp and foreboding. Gingerly, he crossed to stand at the top and stare at the heap at the bottom.

For a moment, he thought of laundry because of the way the clothes were twisted, but he spotted an arm poking this way, a leg that way. Billy wailed again.

Denny grabbed the rail and began to descend. Every step brought him closer, every step made him wonder how could a body be twisted like that? Falling down the stairs in the dark wouldn't do it, but that's what had to have happened. Billy must've fallen.

His hand grasped the big man's shoulder, as if Denny needed to assure himself of Billy's physical reality. The muscle quivered beneath his fingertips. Billy moaned again.

"It's okay, Billy." Denny's voice sounded weak and uncertain, even to his own ears. He cleared his throat. "You must've just slipped in the dark."

Carefully, he worked at straightening his partner's body, no longer caring if his wails brought the police running. Billy's limbs splayed at unnatural angles. His face was twisted and red with pain. Tears coursed down his cheeks. His lips trembled, words coming too softly for Denny to hear. Stooping, he pressed his ear close to Billy's lips.

"Didn't fall, something grabbed," the big man gasped. His voice faded and he breathed heavily through his mouth as though the four words had drained all his strength.

Denny remembered the howl, thought about the oatmeal wall, but that was just craziness, just fantasy, just the dark getting on his nerves. To admit anything else was too big a step for someone as pragmatic as Denny to take. He didn't believe in the bogeyman, didn't believe in haunted houses or vampires or anything like Freddie Kruger. That was movies, make believe.

"There's nobody else here," he said. He forced a confidence he didn't feel into his voice. "You just fell, but don't worry. I'll get you outta here. It'll be all right."

Billy tried to whisper something else but Denny didn't bend down to hear it. He walked toward the kitchen, keeping his pace sure and even. It was an effort not to run.

With Billy as badly wounded as Denny suspected, the job was finished. They'd barely got started, he thought bitterly, but there was no use whining about it. Right now they had to get out and count their blessings.

The back door was properly shut, the ruined lock gapping like a wound. On the waist-high counter along the wall lay the flashlight, just where he'd thought it would be. For reassurance, Denny hefted it in his hand. The best thing to do now would be to get out, take Billy somewhere. He knew people who could help and they didn't ask questions like a hospital would.

He grabbed the door knob and twisted. The knob slid though his fingers, feeling as substantial as gelatin. He tried again. Still he couldn't get a grip, but that didn't matter, the lock was ruined so the door should swing open. He kicked it, expecting it to rebound back. Instead the wood indented, as if made of rubber, then slowly resumed its shape.

Denny's heart pounded inside his thin chest. The door was stuck, something in the lock jammed; that was it. His fingers searched the edges, prying between the door and the door frame. But he couldn't get a grip, couldn't even slip his fingers between the seams. And there had to be seams, it was a door, for god's sake. But his fingers found only a solid seal as if the door had melded to the wall.

"Godammit!" Denny yelled. He pulled out the flashlight and began pounding on the door. Billy's scream stopped him.

Denny froze, the flashlight drooping in his fingers. Billy cried out again, calling to him.

"Denny, help!"

He didn't want to, didn't care anymore about the job or his reputation or his working relationship with Billy. He just wanted out. Billy's scream came again, tightening the skin across Denny's scalp. He clenched the flashlight and crossed to the kitchen door.

The hallway was brightly lit, showing how far Billy had managed to drag his ruined body before he'd stopped, or was stopped. He'd raised himself up on one hand, the other reaching for the wall for support. But Denny could see that Billy was trying to pull away from the wall, could see where his hand disappeared into the flowered wallpaper. A red stain spread over the patterned flowers, and Denny caught a glimpse of bone as Billy jerked away from the wall. His arm suddenly came free, a stump spraying blood where his hand had been. Denny noticed hunks of flesh hanging on the wall. Slowly, they disappeared, as if the wall was absorbing them. Then the stain faded, leaving the flowered wallpaper intact and clean.

Billy fell forward on the hallway throw-rugs, the stump extending toward Denny. Blood pulsed out, soaking into the plush fabric. Billy's eyes rolled up, exposing the whites. He sagged, unconscious. Then his body began rocking and Denny thought he'd been wrong and Billy wasn't unconscious. But as he watched, the pile began shifting, as though blown by an unfelt wind. The pattern of the movement became more like mulching, the edges of the carpet spiking up like teeth. Denny shook his head as the sound of crunching and squishing filled the hallway. Billy's body quivered as the edges of the carpet pierced his skin. As Denny watched, the carpet teeth ground in and Billy began to relax, his body slumping heavier on the carpet. A stain of pinky red and frothy white spread over the fabric, dotted with pieces of Billy's clothes. Dissolving, Denny realized in horror. Billy never regained consciousness as the carpet slowly ate him. The last thing Denny saw was Billy's hand, fingers extended as though reaching for him, before the rug ground it up with the rest. As with the wall, the stain was slowly absorbed.

I'm next, thought Denny wildly. Shit, I'm next!

He ran back to the kitchen but the door was still sealed. Frantically, he pounded on the windows but even the sounds of his pounding were absorbed, muffled. No one outside would be able to hear him.

Keep moving, he thought. He ran through to the dining room and tried to pry the masking tape from the shades, but they too were sealed like the kitchen door. He didn't waste any more time with them and ran into the living room. The windows were the same. He wandered back through the office and remembered the calendar, the circled dates. Today was one of those dates. Had he foolishly thought of coming back here to rob the place again? He'd give anything just to get out now. Then he remembered the pattern of the dates. All the circles were around the time of the full moon. He remembered questioning Billy about lycanthropy. But it wasn't the occupants who were werewolves, it was the house. It was a were-house.

No, that was just crazy.

So was watching your partner being eaten by carpeting.

A prickling sensation on his ankles made him look down. An electric cord wrapped around his pants' leg; was that thorns he saw sticking into the fabric? He tried to pull away. The cord grew taunt and he fell, knocking over a small end table. A potted fern crashed to the carpet beside him. The water made a damp stain by his head.

Fear coursed through Denny. He rolled onto his back and clawed at the cord. It wrapped tighter and he felt his foot fall asleep. Pins and needles started up his calf and thigh. The cord was digging deeper into his pants, into his leg. He felt his skin fray and break, blood oozed over the fabric and dripped on the carpet. It disappeared almost as it hit the pile, as though the carpet was licking it up.

"Let me go!" Denny shouted. "I won't come back, I promise. Just let me go!"

He clawed for the door frame and as his fingers reached the edges of it, the lights went out for good. The creaking started again, building up to another howl. The house wasn't listening anymore.

"Look honey, there's another van in the driveway." The wife pointed as they pulled up in front of the house.

"I guess you were right about that guy who was looking at the house the last couple of months." The husband turned off the ignition.

"Will the bad men be inside the house, mom?" A blonde haired, six-year-old girl peered over the back seat.

"No dear, they'll be gone." She exchanged a look with her husband. "The house will have taken care of them. Why don't we take our bags back into the house while Daddy gets rid of the van?"

She opened the passenger door. "Looks like a nice van," her husband said. "I bet I'll get more for it than the last one."

The wife smiled as she started to hustle the children toward the front door. "Just don't forget carpet cleaner this time. It always smells so damp when we've been gone."

The husband nodded as he walked up the driveway toward the van. "I'll get pine scented. The house seems to like that."

A Walk in The Woods

The old woman woke early on the morning of the thirteenth and lay gazing at the rays of sunlight that filtered through the window. Lying in bed, she felt comfortable and warm. Perhaps today she would walk in the woods alone. She felt well this morning, better than she had in months. She felt like she could run through the woods.

The thought excited her. She sat up in bed, pulling the covers to her face to stifle a giggle. She did not want to wake Gertrude.

She slipped out of bed and began to dress. I must wear warm clothes, she thought, so I will not get sick again.

She moved to the oak chest. Opening it, she selected a white, linen underdress and a heavy green wool skirt. For the top, she picked a grey shirt with matching sweater.

As she dressed, her heart pounded with excitement. Her fingers fumbled with the button on her sweater. Perhaps, she thought, perhaps I can sneak out and back before Gertrude even wakes. This thought threatened to produce more giggles. She hid her face in her hands. Oh this is terrible, she thought, I shouldn't go to the woods.

Lifting her hand mirror, she traced the lines on her face with a thin finger.

"I should not go to the woods," she whispered to her reflection. Her reflection was not convinced. She looked healthy, radiant. A walk in the woods surely would not make her ill.

"I will go to the woods," she said defiantly. "Whether Gertrude likes it or not."

Suddenly she glanced back at the door. *You shouldn't have spoken aloud, idiot,* she scolded herself in silence. She smiled one last time at her reflection, holding it to its secret promise then inched towards the door.

The hallway beyond lay silent and cool. She slipped across it to the stairway. The lower level was shrouded in darkness. Gertrude was not to be seen.

She forced herself to tiptoe down the stairs. The urge to shout happily and dash away before Gertrude caught her was almost overwhelming. With difficulty, she restrained herself.

As she eased down the stairs, she avoided the seventeenth step which creaked. Suddenly a soft noise of something behind her caught her attention. She froze and glanced back. Sunlight shone from the window at the top of the stairs. A branch brushed lazily against the glass.

She let out her breath in a sigh of relief, realizing only then that she'd held it.

"Silly," she whispered to herself. She crept down the remaining stairs and crossed the darkened entrance hall. As she slipped on her brown shoes, she contemplated whether she should take a cloak.

No, she thought mischievously, it's warm enough without a cloak and I have my sweater. Grinning, she snuck to the door. With one final glance, she giggled and left.

The air smelled crisp and fresh, entirely different from the stale old air of her room. She smiled as she took a deep breath and stepped outside. The walkway felt good under her feet and the sun warmed on her face.

I'm alive, she thought, I am alive.

A path branched off from the walkway and wove its way through the grounds to the edge of the woods. Without hesitation, she took the path.

How brave I'm getting, she marveled. If Gertrude sees me and shouts I shan't pay any attention. I'll pretend I didn't hear her. What could she do?

She snickered and hurried slightly. The woods were a fair distance away. A breeze rustled the branches and she fancied they were waving her to come forward.

The trees stood tall and strong. The bark of the trunks and branches felt rough and coarse beneath her fingers. Dark green leaves waved in the breeze. Deep, lush brown earth lay covered with a scattering of moss and undergrowth.

She hesitated only a moment before she entered, the old fear of Gertrude resurfacing. The crabby servant scared the old woman with her harsh, prying eyes. The old woman's daughter had hired Gertrude; she'd had no say in the matter. She always felt intimidated by Gertrude, resentful of the servant's superior attitude. "You're too old to help here," Gertrude would say when the old woman tried to help in the kitchen. "You're too old to carry things," Gertrude would say when the old woman tried to lift some wood. According to Gertrude, she was too old to do anything but whither away.

But she wouldn't let today be spoiled. She pushed the feeling away and stepped into the woods, her head held high. The trees rustled almost saying hello. As she stepped between the trunks and underbrush, it was as though the woods had swallowed her whole.

She was in her domain now; she was at home. As her feet moved along the ground, the thought of Gertrude and her disapproving daughter faded from her mind.

Strolling boldly down the winding path, she moved deep into the heart of the woods. She felt young again, almost like the little girl in the story who set off through the woods and got chased by large, ferocious wolves. Everything worked out in the end for that little girl. The wolves were driven off by a strong, friendly man and the little girl reached her destination. She smiled at the thought. Her father used to tell her those stories endlessly, repeating the ones she loved best. She used to pretend she didn't know the end and was scared. He hugged her and stroked her hair, promising that the wolves would never get her. She felt safe with father, feeling his strong arms around her. No wolf could come close.

She bent over and plucked a wild flower. She always wondered what happened to those wolves; they were driven off at the end of the story but never quite destroyed. Perhaps they returned to the forest to wait for new little girls to terrify.

She stopped by a small creek and sat on a log to watch its progression. The tiny music of the creek soothed her, filling her with tranquility and calm. She was so glad she had come. The scent of the breeze was fresh and light. She admired the beauty of the trees soaring above her head, a quilt of colors and shadows. Subtle sounds of the woods reached her ears, creaks and tweets and rustling and hissing and scraping, whispering of life and adventures. It was so peaceful. A smile played across her dry lips. She closed her eyes and breathed deeply.

When she shook herself awake it was almost dark. She looked around, for a moment disoriented. Oh yes, she remembered now. It must be dreadfully late, she noticed. Gertrude would be furious. Goodness, she'd be late for dinner, and her daughter was visiting tonight. Flustered, she struggled to her feet and started back in the direction of the house.

Her legs were sore and uncooperative. She tried to shake and rub the life back into them, to force them to hurry but they still moved so slowly. Oh, how she hated being old and worn out.

Her breath sounded hard and deep. She felt her chest heaving as she moved. Then she noticed something strange. Odd how the breathing she heard didn't match the movement of her chest. She stopped and listened. The breathing came from some point behind her. It sounded heavy, almost a growl instead of a breath. The smell reached her a moment later, a foul, hot stench that clutched at her throat. She froze suddenly in fear. What in the world was that? She certainly didn't want to find out.

Now she began to hurry along the path, forcing her legs faster, no longer worried about Gertrude or dinner. The thing behind her sounded like some sort of beast, and it was gaining on her; she heard its breath quicken with interest.

She sobbed once and tried to coax more speed from her sore and stiffening legs. The breathing became a growl, low and intense as the thing sensed prey. God, what could it be? It almost sounded like a...wolf?

There were no wolves in this part of the forest, she was certain of it. It was impossible. Just impossible.

Suddenly the thing howled, a horrendous, screeching sound that ripped through the air. She felt it right behind her. She screamed and ran. Her legs stopped cooperating. She stumbled, righted herself and limped on. Her feet landed heavy on the ground, thumping like cement, almost too heavy to lift. Her thighs cramped. One calf ached, pain piercing up her leg. She whimpered but forced herself to keep going, keep going! She sensed rather than felt a paw or arm rise up and strike down toward her. She tried to run faster. Her old body just didn't have the energy to respond. Something heavy landed on her back. She crashed to the forest floor.

Dazed, she opened her eyes and struggled vainly to untangle her body. One of her shoes lay in a clump of bushes off to her left. A tiny part of her mind focused on it, reminding her that Gertrude would scold her for getting mud on them. Slowly, she shifted her eyes up to the advancing monster and gasped.

It was a wolf, or at least wolf-like. It reared up on two legs, using the front legs as arms. Coarse dark hair matted with dirt covered its head and hands. Saliva dripped from the open mouth.

The old woman opened her mouth to scream when the wolf-thing reached up a paw and pulled its face off.

"See what happens when you don't listen to me?" Gertrude shouted. She glared down at the old woman and dropped the mask at her feet. "I told you these woods weren't safe."

She grabbed the old woman's hands to help her to her feet. The old woman stared at the mask, obviously an actor's prop in the dirt. How could she have been fooled?

"Come on, you have disrupted my day," the servant said scornfully. She turned to lead the way out of the woods.

The air hissed and there was a flash of motion. Gertrude fell without a cry. The old woman blinked and staggered back a step.

An old man in a brown tunic and worn pants limped out of the surrounding bushes, dragging a large axe. The blade was bloody.

He tipped his hat to the old woman. "Sorry to scare you, milady, but I couldn't let that wolf take you. Not when you need to get to your grandmother's house."

Before the old woman could reply, he raised the axe over his head and swung, slicing Gertrude's head off with one clean stroke. The head skidded along the ground, coming to rest beside her shoe.

At least now, Gertrude couldn't scold her about the mud.

Wolf's Bane

Mrs. Willis was a deep sleeper and didn't hear the phone until the fifth ring. Blinking, she sputtered awake, her voice a gravely beast in her throat as she croaked, "Fred, can you get that?"

The phone continued to ring. Must have gone to the shop early, Mrs. Willis thought fuzzily. She stumbled out of bed and groped into the hall.

"Hello?"

"Eva, is that you?"

Mrs. Willis sighed. "Of course, it's me, Joan. Who else would it be?"

"Oh yes, well, have you seen Fred today?"

Mrs. Willis rubbed sleep from her eyes. Being woken from a deep sleep didn't give her a good temperament for twenty questions.

"No, Joan, he's probably left for the shop."

"Oh, um, well, okay, it's probably nothing then."

Mrs. Willis closed her eyes and ran a hand through her greying hair. Take a deep breath, Eva, she told herself.

"What's nothing, Joan?"

"Oh well, Eva, I was just getting a snack last night. Felt a bit peckish and thought some soup would soothe my nerves..."

Mrs. Willis's fist tightened in her hair. Her jaw clenched. If Joan Davis stood in front of her right now she didn't know if she could resist the temptation to bite her square on her fat nose. Be calm, she reminded herself. Her mother had always told her that a bad temper wasn't lady-like.

"I usually like tomato but that's a little acidic, so I thought..."

"Joan!"

"Oh yes, um, right. So I was down in the

kitchen and I heard a car driving by. Not very fast, rather slow actually. In fact, it stopped, outside the house. I saw it when I looked out the living room window."

"Well, that's a great story, Joan," Mrs. Willis said. "I really have to be going."

"No, wait, Eva. The truck, I saw writing on it. It said 'Dog Catcher.'"

Mrs. Willis dropped the phone.

She checked the entire house, including the sub-basement with the crawl space in front and the attic. Nothing, nada, zip. Standing in the hallway, dust bunnies from the basement tangled in her hair, Mrs. Willis clutched her flannel nightgown to her chest.

Oh god, a dog catcher.

Hadn't they moved from the city to avoid them, the pound, the Humane Society? Can't enter this park without a leash, poop'n scoop, every dog must have a license and shots. They'd specifically moved out of Toronto to avoid the traps. Now...

Fred, oh Fred.

Why didn't you wake me, she thought, staring at the heavy leather leash that hung on a nail outside the bedroom door. But she knew the answer to that one.

Fred didn't like to be a bother.

There was still time, it was still early. Just after seven. The sun was only now giving some consideration to rising, but it wouldn't make up its mind to start for at least half an hour.

Mrs. Willis hunched over the steering wheel of the old Honda. The traffic was unbelievable, even at this early hour. She had to refrain from blaring her horn at every idiot that got in the way. Getting a ticket for reckless driving wasn't going to help.

Why did the pound have to be so far from her house? She'd gotten the address from information. A new place, just opened a week ago. Wonderful. A new county ordinance. Well, she knew what she thought of their new ordinance. She imagined Fred would be quite graphic in his display.

The traffic crept along until she thought she was going to go mad. Finally her turnoff became visible in the distance. A fast check of her watch told her it was seven twenty. She tapped her wedding band on the steering wheel.

If her mother knew about this she'd be snickering right now, Mrs. Willis knew. She'd always disapproved of Fred, too wild, too impulsive for his own good. Of course, she didn't know the half of it. But after growing up the daughter of a reverend and with a mother determined to protect her from the stress and evils of the world, Mrs. Willis found she needed some wildness in her life. Fred's enthusiasm was just right and she'd supported him, even through the toughest times.

The turnoff, finally. She began to relax as she sped along the county road, leaving the clog of the highway behind. No radar traps here. She'd reach the pound with time to spare. Load Fred into the back seat and cover him up with the blanket for the ride home. The back windows were frosted so no one would be able to see in. Safe.

The pound was a tiny grey building set a ways back from the road. Mrs. Willis parked in the gravel parking lot in front. As she got out of the car, a chorus of barks drifted out from behind the building. That's where the pens are, she thought, clasping her purse to her breast. She listened for a moment, but couldn't discern Fred's voice.

The front door was locked but there was a buzzer next to it. Mrs. Willis leaned into it, listening to the echo behind the door. After a moment, a man's voice shouted.

"Alright, I'm coming!"

She released the buzzer and waited. Seconds crawled by until she began to root to the spot, the seasons changing around her as the days passed. Wind ruffled her hair, and she imagined it was the beginning of winter now although it was spring when she'd first set out. Then the door sprang open.

A hulking man peered down at her with bleary eyes. "Yeah?"

"I think you picked up my dog last night," Mrs. Willis said. "I've come to claim him."

The man blinked at her, then rubbed a hand over his bristly cheek. "Come in."

She followed him into the tiny waiting room and stood in front of the Formica counter while he crossed to the back. He opened a ledger and peered down at it. Mrs. Willis waited, resisting the impulse to tap her foot. She couldn't let the man see how impatient she was, how desperate.

"What kinda dog?" he asked.

"A mongrel really," she said. "Big, grey all over, long hair. Light blue eyes."

"Must have some husky in 'em," the man grunted. He turned a page casually in the ledger. Mrs. Willis restrained herself from digging her nails into his hand to make him move faster. Be calm, she thought. Her mother's warnings about the evils of stress flittered through her mind. She took deep breaths.

"Don't see anything in the ledger. Let me check the night receipts in the back office."

He turned away from her, shoving his hands in his pockets, not bothering to look up at her. Not only slow but rude as well, she thought. What was happening to courtesy these days? She peered over the counter top to look at the ledger. He'd conveniently closed it. How long would he be back in the office? Maybe she could take a quick peek.

The book was heavier than she thought and the pages flapped when she tried to pick it up.

A card fluttered out, landing on the counter. Quickly she snatched it up, about to stuff it back into the book.

"Richmond Breeders," the card read. Mrs. Willis clutched the card.

The dog catcher shuffled in from the back room. "Sorry, lady, didn't pick up any big mutts last night." He shrugged to emphasize the point.

He still wouldn't look at her. "Thank you for your help," Mrs. Willis said formally. She turned and walked precisely to her car.

Only when she'd started the engine and driven out of the parking lot and onto the county road again did she take the card from her pocket and read the address.

"Richmond Breeders," she murmured to herself. The address was almost an hour's drive. She swallowed, her fingertips whitening where she gripped the card.

She prayed she wouldn't be too late.

Fred Willis blinked at the bars of the pen. Even without a window he knew the sun was rising, he could feel it in his bones. They wanted to shift and stretch like a sleeping person upon awakening. But he was locked inside this pen and he couldn't allow himself to change now. Not when there would be witnesses. Not when she was here.

He stared over at the tall, dark brown bitch that curled up against the far wall of the pen. She noticed him looking at her and raised her sleek head. Quickly he looked away, scratching half heartedly at the dirt floor. He didn't want to have to fend her off again.

God, this was terrible, he thought, and embarrassing. If only he hadn't been so obsessed with that bloody squirrel he would have noticed the dog catcher and escaped. Now he was stuck here, in some breeder's pen, expected to do... To do.... He shuddered.

Of course, the worst thing was that the bitch tantalized him. Intellectually he knew it was merely pheromones; the bitch was in heat, but he couldn't deny that the idea had some allure and he felt ashamed. Imagine at his age, thinking such thoughts, it was disgraceful! And what about Eva? They had a wonderful marriage and he never thought of cheating on her. But the breeder had already come back in twice, angry that nothing had happened yet. Fred had no idea what would happen if he came in a third time.

Could this even be defined as cheating? he wondered. He looked over at the bitch again. She was watching him, but didn't move, her head resting on her forepaws. She was just a dog, he knew, he could tell she wasn't like him. Could such a thing be considered adultery? It wasn't like he had many options.

Footsteps on the stairs raised the fur on his neck. Impulsively he growled low in his throat. He'd tried to cooperate with these people but it hadn't gotten him anywhere. Maybe it was time for some of the old fire.

Two men entered the basement wearing thick gloves and leather pants. The shorter one held a dart gun. The snarl died in Fred's throat. His heart pounded in his furry chest. Oh god, they meant to kill him, just because he hadn't...

"You sure about this?" the dark haired one asked. He gestured toward Fred.

The short man fiddled with the gun.

"Guaranteed. This stuff would even get you started. Maybe I should sell some to your wife."

"Very funny. Just do it."

The gun aimed at Fred. Fred stood transfixed, staring at the barrel. He knew he should move, try to dodge, but while he was still considering it the gun spat. A needle pierced his shoulder and he yelped. Fire poured into his veins. With a snarl, Fred bit at the needle then lunged at the pen bars. The two men jumped back. The first one grinned.

"Seems pretty energetic now."

"Yeah, just you wait and see."

For Fred, the world began to tilt. He heard the men talking but it was white noise, nothing significant. He staggered away from the bars, trying to turn toward the back. He felt like he did when he had one too many beers at McMurphy's Pub.

The bitch rose and took at step toward him. Her musky smell enveloped him, strong and succulent. Fred blinked and tried to bark. It came out as a worble. Behind him, the men laughed.

Maybe it wasn't such a bad idea, he thought, looking at the bitch's sleek head, her muscular body. She wasn't a bad looking dog. Good teeth. Maybe just for a minute. Fred took a step.

The doorbell rang.

Mrs. Willis rang the bell again for good measure. She checked her watch for the tenth time, it was still eight forty-five.

Fred had to be here, she thought desperately. She didn't have any real proof, just the business card and her own instincts which had encouraged her the whole time she drove. She'd sped all the way, luckily avoiding any police. That too felt like confirmation. He was here, she could feel it.

Sort of.

Should she ring a third time? What if she was wrong and these people were asleep in their beds and she was rudely awakening them? She bit her lower lip. That guilt only added to her burden, making her shoulders hunch. This much stress was not good for her, not good for her constitution.

The door snatched open before her. Startled, Mrs. Willis gasped. A tall lanky man wearing leather pants and a tight dark shirt glared at her.

"Yeah?"

"Oh, I'm sorry to disturb you." Mrs. Willis struggled to regain her composure. "I understand you received a large grey dog from the Country dog catcher this morning."

If she'd guessed wrong, the man would simply deny it and then what? Nervously, she swallowed, twining her fingers in her purse strap.

"Sorry lady, we bought the mutt fair and square. Paid a good penny too. You'll have to take it up with the dog catcher."

Fred was here! "But you bought him illegally. I'm sure we could get the dog catcher to reimburse you."

"Forget it. It's your problem and he's my dog." He started to close the door.

Desperately, Mrs. Willis put her hand out to stop him.

"Wait, please, I'd be willing to pay."

The man rolled his eyes. "Go get another mutt, lady, I got plans for this one. Don't come here again or I'll charge you with trespassing." A nasty grin lit up the young man's thin face. "And don't bother going to the police either. All they'll find is doggy chops."

With a chuckle, he slammed the door in her face.

Mrs. Willis clutched her purse. Tears stung her eyes. Fred was here and no matter what vulgar things that young man said she wasn't going to let them keep Fred without a fight.

With a determined sniff, she set off to scout around the house.

"Who was that?"

The words sounded all strung together to Fred, a jumble of syllables. It helped to clear his head of the ringing he still heard.

"Some old bat looking for her dog," commented the man as he descended the stairs. He gestured loosely at the pen.

Fred, who had turned to advance on the bitch again, stopped short. The second man's words had sounded more distinct. Old bat. What did that mean? His mind felt fuzzy. Growling, he shook his head. He should remember, somehow he knew that. Old bat.

Eva!

The adrenaline rush the thought of her caused was too much for Fred. Too late he recognized the familiar tingling in his toes. Normally he could maintain his form for almost a full day if necessary, but this situation was anything but normal.

Fred let out a howl which shifted octaves to become a moan.

Dimly he was aware of the two men running toward the pen, shouting. But it was no longer important as his body began to transform. Fire raced through his body as his legs muscles shifted. Bones snapped under the internal pressure, grinding into a new configuration. His fur fell out in clumps, leaving his skin raw and itchy. Dimly he remembered how Eva had always stood at the ready with a full bottle of Vaseline intensive care lotion.

Snorting, he wiped fur from his eyes and stared through the bars at the two men. Both stood open mouthed, faces flushed with excitement and fear. In the far corner of the pen, the bitch cowered and whined. In a burst of movement, the younger man jumped back and scooped up his gun.

Fred staggered to his feet. His mouth tasted like gravel and fur. He coughed and tried to speak.

The younger man raised the gun. But a shadow moved on the stairs behind him and a beer case crashed down onto his head. The man dropped, the gun skidding across the floor.

Fred gripped the bars of the cage door and pushed. Metal groaned but didn't give. He had to try harder; soon he would be fully human with only the strength of an old man.

From the shadows on the stairway, Mrs. Willis stepped down. She dropped the beer case onto the body of the younger man. Across him, she faced the lanky man with leather pants.

"I told you he's mine," she snapped.

The lanky man lunged for the gun. Mrs Willis swung her purse to block him.

Fred's heart pounded in his chest. Vaguely he was aware of the bitch behind him, whining eagerly. With one final push, the bars snapped, spilling Fred onto the floor. The bitch leapt out after him.

He rolled and bounced to his feet, a foot away from where the man was aiming at Eva. At Eva! Rage flooded Fred, making his lips draw back from his teeth in a snarl.

His nails, still more claw than nail, sliced through

the man's forearm, exposing slick muscle and bone. The man shrieked, numb fingers dropping the gun. He fell a moment later to his knees, clutching his ruined arm against him. The bitch jumped forward, snapping.

Fred turned to see Mrs Willis' white face. She gulped in air. He crossed to her and took her arm.

"It's all right, dear. You mustn't strain yourself."

She nodded and took several deep breaths. "I'm fine now, dear."

He patted her cheek and turned back to the groaning man.

"I don't know if you can hear me," he said. "But this is the consequences of your thoughtless actions. Your arm will heal, but you'll be changed from now on."

"Fred," Mrs Willis interrupted.

"Yes, dear?"

She fiddled with her belt, a sure sign that she had something unpleasant to say. "I don't think he should. I mean, he's not a very nice man."

Fred pursed his lips. He couldn't just kill the man, not like this. He would be no better than these hoodlums.

"What else can we do, Eva?"

A smile touched her wrinkled face, reminding him of her smile so long ago, on a smooth face full of trust and love.

"I think there's someone else here who deserves it more."

She reached out and patted the bitch's head. The bitch wagged her tail, trying to nuzzle the old woman's hand. Mrs Willis chuckled.

"She's so friendly," she said. "I hate the thought of giving her to that wretched dog catcher. He lied to me about finding you. Imagine what he would do to her." She scratched the dog's throat. The dog closed her eyes with pleasure.

"Besides," Mrs Willis continued. "You'll need someone to look after you when you hunt. Goodness knows you can't do it yourself."

Fred studied the dog. He'd never changed an animal before. "She'll need a lot of food for a few days," he said. "I don't think we have anything at home."

"Oh Fred, don't be silly," Mrs Willis said. "There's plenty here for her."

"Of course," Fred said. "Hold her still, will you, dear?"

Afterward, Mrs Willis helped Fred up the basement stairs to the kitchen. As he sat at the table, she puttered around, looking for items to make tea. It was almost like being at home, as if they'd woken normally.

"I have such a headache," Fred said.

"Yes dear, you've had a most traumatic night," Mrs Willis said, and to soothe her husband's nerves, she turned on the radio loudly to drown out the sound of flesh ripping and the lanky man's final screams.

About the Author

Based in Toronto, Canada, Rebecca M. Senese writes horror, science fiction and mystery/crime, often all at once in the same story. Garnering an Honorable Mention in "The Year's Best Science Fiction" and nominated for numerous Aurora Awards, her work has appeared in *Tesseracts 16: Parnassus Unbound, Imaginarium 2012, Tesseracts 15: A Case of Quite Curious Tales, Ride the Moon, TransVersions, Deadbolt Magazine, On Spec, The Vampire's Crypt, Storyteller, Reflection's Edge, Future Syndicate* and *Into the Darkness*, amongst others.

When not serving up tales of the macabre, mysterious or wondrous, she volunteers as a zombie or vampire at haunted attractions in October to stalk and scare all the unsuspecting innocents.

Find Me Online

Website - http://www.RebeccaSenese.com
Twitter - http://twitter.com/RebeccaSenese